Olga Meets Her Match

OTHER YEARLING BOOKS YOU WILL ENJOY:

THE TALES OF OLGA DA POLGA, *Michael Bond*

OLGA CARRIES ON, *Michael Bond*

OLGA TAKES CHARGE, *Michael Bond*

A BEAR CALLED PADDINGTON, *Michael Bond*

PADDINGTON MARCHES ON, *Michael Bond*

PADDINGTON AT LARGE, *Michael Bond*

PADDINGTON AT WORK, *Michael Bond*

PADDINGTON GOES TO TOWN, *Michael Bond*

PADDINGTON HELPS OUT, *Michael Bond*

PADDINGTON ON TOP, *Michael Bond*

YEARLING BOOKS are designed especially to entertain and enlighten young people. Charles F. Reasoner, Professor Emeritus of Children's Literature and Reading, New York University, is consultant to this series.

For a complete listing of all Yearling titles,
write to Education Sales Department, Dell Publishing Co., Inc.,
1 Dag Hammarskjold Plaza, New York, New York 10017.

Olga Meets Her Match

MICHAEL BOND

ILLUSTRATED BY HANS HELWEG

A YEARLING BOOK

Published by
Dell Publishing Co., Inc.
1 Dag Hammarskjold Plaza
New York, New York 10017

This work is published simultaneously in a hardcover volume entitled
The Complete Adventures of Olga da Polga by Delacorte Press, New York,
New York.

Olga Meets Her Match was first published in Great Britain by Kestrel Books.

Text copyright © 1973 by Michael Bond

Illustrations copyright © 1973 by Hans Helweg

Yearling® TM 913705, Dell Publishing Co., Inc.

ISBN: 0-440-46622-9

Printed in the United States of America

First Yearling printing—April 1983

CW

CONTENTS

1   *Olga Goes Away*   7

2   *A Strange Meeting*   19

3   *Boris's Story*   29

4   *A Rude Awakening*   42

5   *Olga Solves a Mystery*   50

6   *The Night of the Long Dance*   62

7   *Olga Takes the Plunge*   72

8   *Olga Gets Her Own Back*   85

9   *Olga to the Rescue*   95

10 *Olga and the Chinese Dragon*   108

11 *A Day to Remember*   119

CHAPTER ONE

Olga Goes Away

Olga da Polga wasn't feeling well. She was far from being her usual self, and she hadn't been her usual self for several weeks.

Her condition was causing the Sawdust family a great deal of concern, and one morning Mr Sawdust decided something would have to be done about it.

Pausing on his way to work, he peered through the door of Olga's hutch and took a long, hard look at the ball of brown and white fur huddled deep inside the hay.

'If you ask me,' he said, 'that guinea-pig needs

taking out of herself. Look at her – she hasn't moved for days. A change of air – that's what she needs.'

A second figure joined him outside the wire netting. 'It might be worth a try.' Mrs Sawdust sounded slightly doubtful about the idea. 'As long as it isn't a change for the worse.'

'Well, we must do *something*,' said Mr Sawdust briskly. 'The whole thing's been going on far too long. We'll take a trip to the sea-side this week-end. There's nothing like a good, stiff sea-breeze through your whiskers when you're feeling low. It'll make a new animal of her.'

Olga stirred as the muffled voices filtered through the hay. For a moment or two she wondered if her ears were working properly – so much of her wasn't these days. She'd never even heard of a sea-side before, and as for being made into a new animal . . .

Scrambling to her feet she hurried into the dining-room to protest. 'Wheeeee!' she shrieked at the top of her voice. 'Wheeeeeee! I don't want to be made into a new animal, thank you very much. I like being a guinea-pig.'

But she had left it too late. Mr and Mrs Sawdust were nowhere in sight and Olga found herself addressing the empty air.

For a moment or two she stared indignantly at the

spot where they'd been. Then, partly because the excitement had suddenly made her feel hungry, but also because she wanted to make matters harder for

anyone who tried to tamper with her present arrangements, she turned to her food bowl.

Olga could be very difficult when she chose, and she ate an unusually hearty breakfast by any standards. When she had finished her oats she polished off a large pile of grass, and then rounded things off by eating several dandelions followed by two halves of a freshly split carrot for good measure.

'Just let them try making a new animal out of me now,' she gasped. 'Just let them try.'

Olga's stomach felt as tight as a drum. It was as much as she could do to drag herself back into her bedroom, and once there she sank down into the hay with a sigh of relief.

It was the first proper meal she'd had in ages, and
if her eyes had been bigger than her stomach to begin
with they certainly weren't now.

Olga's poor health was mostly the fault of the weather. The winter had been long and damp, and towards
the end of it she had caught a nasty cold which had left
her feeling weak and listless. Her fur had lost its usual
gloss and she hardly bothered to keep herself tidy,
which was most unusual.

The Sawdust family had taken her to the vet several
times, and on his advice they'd tried mixing a few
drops of cod liver oil in with her oats, but as she'd
hardly been near her food bowl this had been of no
help at all.

Gradually the unexpected meal began to have its
effect. Olga's eyelids grew heavier and heavier and she
sank deeper and deeper into her hay, until in no time at
all she was fast asleep again.

How long she stayed that way Olga didn't know, but when she woke it was to the sound of yet another voice. This time it belonged to Karen Sawdust.

'Perhaps it isn't the cold at all,' she was saying. 'Perhaps she just needs company. She looks very lonely all by herself.'

'If that's the case,' said Mrs Sawdust meaningly, 'the sooner we make a move the better.'

'Oh, dear,' said Karen Sawdust. 'I do hope she doesn't fade away before we get there. Animals do that sometimes. They stop eating and lose the will to live and they simply fade away.'

Olga put on her most woebegone expression ever as the door of her hutch swung open. 'That's it,' she groaned to herself. 'I'm fading away. I expect if I looked in my drinking bowl now I wouldn't be able to see myself in the water I'm so faded.'

'*Fading away?*' exclaimed Mr Sawdust as he reached inside and picked her up. 'You must be joking!' He

squeezed Olga's stomach, gently but firmly. 'Feel that! Solid as a rock. And look at her bowl of oats – she's been through the lot. I reckon she's been having us on.'

Olga stared up at the others in disgust. 'You should have squeezed me this morning,' she thought. 'Or *tried* to more like it. You wouldn't have been able to then there was so little of me.'

Olga was so upset by the remarks being passed about her she scarcely noticed what was happening, and it wasn't until she took a deep breath and gathered her senses again that she realized she was sitting in a cardboard box.

Not only that, but in the background she could hear the sound of an engine.

She was sitting in a cardboard box in a motor car. And that could only mean one thing. She was being taken somewhere.

Suddenly it all came back to her. She was going to the sea-side!

Usually the thought of doing anything new filled her with excitement, but in her present state all it did was make her wish more than ever that she hadn't eaten quite so much. She was glad the Sawdust family had thought to line the box with hay, for it stopped her banging against the side when the car went round corners, and after her heavy meal Olga was in no fit state to bang against anything.

She lay where she was for a while, listening to the drone of the engine and to the sound of voices.

Karen Sawdust's voice floated through the hole in the lid of the box first. 'I've packed her case,' she said. 'There's a bagful of grass – in case she doesn't like it where she's going. And some oats, and some cod liver oil, and her own water bowl . . .' The voice paused for a moment and an eye appeared at the hole above Olga's

head. 'I wonder what it's like, being taken everywhere in a cardboard box?'

'Hmmmm,' said Olga to herself. 'You may well ask. I might not even have *wanted* to go.'

'She may not even have wanted to go,' persisted Karen Sawdust. 'I wish we could read her thoughts.'

Olga began to feel very superior. 'You may not be able to read *my* thoughts,' she squeaked. 'But I can read yours!'

'I suppose,' broke in Mr Sawdust, 'it's much the same as if a great big giant came along and picked one of *us* up. Rather frightening.'

'Not if it was a nice giant,' said Karen Sawdust. 'One you could trust and you *knew* wouldn't harm you. One who always took you to nice places – like the sea-side. Oh, I *do* wish I knew what she's thinking.'

But by then Olga wasn't really thinking anything at all. She'd been with the Sawdust family for so long now it didn't need any talk about giants – nice or nasty – for her to know they wouldn't let any harm come to her. The heavy meal and the warmth of the car were making her feel sleepy again. And the experience of riding through the countryside was no longer new. She'd done it so many times before it was really rather boring. Everything went past at such a speed it was impossible to take it all in, and once you've seen one field you've seen the lot – especially if you can't stop and nibble it.

It was dark when Olga woke. At least, dark wasn't quite the right word; for it was a dark with lights on. Brightly coloured lights. Red lights, blue lights, green lights; lights of many different colours, hanging just

above her head almost as if the sky had suddenly closed
in on them.

She scrambled to her feet, hoping for a better look.
'Wherever have I got to now?' she breathed.

Licking her lips in anticipation, she gave a start and
then licked them again. They had a strange, yet
somehow very familiar taste. She'd come across it
before somewhere. Then she remembered. It was
called *salt*. That was it – salt. She'd once stepped in
some by accident when she'd been left in the Sawdust
family's kitchen while her own house was being
cleaned out. And now the air was full of it.

'Well, Olga?' Karen lifted up the lid of the box so that she could have a better view. 'You're at the sea-side now. What do you think of it?'

'Wheeeeee!' Olga gave an excited squeak as she peered over the edge. 'I'm at the sea-side. And it's got lots of coloured lights and it tastes salty and...'

She pricked up her ears as a roaring sound filled the air. It was like nothing she had ever heard before; al-most as if someone was pouring an enormous pile of stones out of a sack.

'There's the sea!' exclaimed Karen Sawdust. She tilted the box a little more. 'Look at all the waves breaking on the shore.'

Olga gave another squeak, partly with delight, partly with fear, as she saw a huge white-topped wall of water rushing towards her.

'Wheeeee!' she shrieked. 'Wheeeeeeeee! I'm going to get wheeeeeeett... I know I am... I...'

But Olga didn't get wet, for the wall of water suddenly appeared to change its mind, and with a deep sighing roar it collapsed in a heap on the beach. Olga never did know what happened to it after that, for just then Mr Sawdust did something to the car and they turned down a side street away from the sea.

She wasn't sure whether to feel pleased or sorry, but

as it happened she didn't really have time to feel either. A moment later they drew to a halt outside a large house and she felt her box bobbing up and down once more as the family climbed out of the car.

A light went on and for the next few minutes the air was alive with a babble of strange voices. Olga couldn't make out much of what was going on, but from the little she could understand it seemed they were staying with friends and that she, Olga, had a house of her own all ready for her.

'Fancy having a house of my own at the sea-side!' she breathed. 'Whatever next?'

But the 'whatever next' turned out to be something even Olga hadn't bargained on. She caught sight of it as she was being put into her room. It was written in large letters above the door. Just one word, but it set her mind awhirl.

After the others had gone Olga lay quite still for a long while thinking about it. She was so used to seeing her own name – OLGA DA POLGA – painted above her own front door she could still hardly believe she'd seen aright. But she knew she had. 'B – O – R – I – S' it had said. BORIS!

And then in a sudden blinding flash it came to her. 'They've made a new animal of me after all!' she squeaked. 'They've made a new animal of me – and

it didn't hurt a bit. In fact,' she ran round and round her hutch several times just to make doubly sure, 'I think I feel better already!'

CHAPTER TWO

A Strange Meeting

Olga slept well that night, better than she had for a long time, and when she woke the following morning she felt unusually refreshed.

'How nice to be brand new again!' she squeaked, as she hurried into her dining-room.

Peering into the water bowl she half expected to see some strange new face staring back at her, but it looked much the same as usual.

'They've probably kept the best of the old,' she thought. 'And very wise of them too. I don't think I would really like to change that much and not be recognized.'

She ate a hearty breakfast, for the sea air was already having its effect, and then she sat back in order to study her new surroundings.

Her holiday house was not unlike the one she had with the Sawdust family. A little more cramped perhaps, and not quite as well cared for, but really very pleasant. Things weren't in their proper place, of course. But then other people's never were. The food bowl was on the wrong side of the dining-room for a start, but a few good shoves soon put that right. And the sawdust wasn't scattered entirely to her liking, but again that was quickly attended to.

Her housework done for the day, Olga turned her attention to the view through the window. Rather disappointingly, she couldn't actually see the sea, but in the distance she could distinctly make out the sound of waves breaking on the shore. And the smell of the sea was all around her. In the air, in the hay, even in the food she ate.

At the back of the house there was a lawn and a flower bed, and beyond that a strange low building quite unlike anything she had ever seen before.

It seemed to be made of stone and it covered quite a large area. The surrounding walls were about the same height as her own garden run at home, and apart from the main building, which stood at the far end, there were a number of towers, each one a miniature castle in itself.

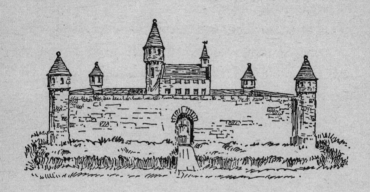

The whole area was covered by wire-netting – either to keep other animals out or to keep *something* in, and Olga spent some time wondering what on earth it could be.

In an odd kind of way it made her feel homesick, for she felt sure that given half a chance she could weave many a fanciful tale about the place, and the more she thought about it the more she wished that one or other of her friends – Noel the cat, or Fangio the hedgehog or even Graham the tortoise, had come with her on holiday so that she could try some of them out.

Tales of princesses locked in one of the towers – perhaps even a whole family of princesses – one in each

tower, kept from ever seeing each other by some creature who lived in the big house.

Olga's imagination began to run riot. 'If only,'
she thought, 'if only I could have a peep inside. Just
one peep, that's all I ask.'

And then, hardly had the thought left her mind, than
the strangest thing happened. A shadow crossed in
front of the window, there was a click as the door catch
was opened, and Karen Sawdust came into view.

'Olga,' she said, holding out both hands palms
uppermost to make a cradle, 'I hope you're on
your best behaviour today. You're going out
visiting.'

'Visiting?' Olga's heart began to beat faster as she
felt herself being carried across the lawn.

'The *castle*!' she squeaked excitedly. 'Wheeeee!
I'm going to visit the castle. The Sawdust people must
be able to read my thoughts after all!'

For a moment or two it all seemed too good to be
true. But then, as they drew near, she began to have
second thoughts.

The castle was surrounded by a kind of moat, and the
only way in – or *out* – appeared to be by means of a
plank of wood which led to a small door let into the
side of one of the walls. Closer to, it looked somewhat
dark and forbidding and she would have been per-

fectly happy to let matters rest there. A peep was one thing, but actually going inside such a place was quite another matter. In fact, if she'd had a tail to turn Olga would have turned it then and there and made a run for it. But she'd left things much too late. Before she could utter a single squeak of protest Karen Sawdust bent down, slid the door open, and Olga felt herself being bundled through the opening.

As the door slid shut behind her she crouched where she was, as still as the very stone the castle was made of, while she took careful stock of her new surroundings.

It was much brighter inside than she had expected. The walls were painted white, and rather unexpectedly the floor was made of grass.

After a moment or two, Olga plucked up courage and had a quick nibble. It was rather nice grass. Not quite the sort she'd been used to. For one thing it was too salty for her taste, but really . . . she took another nibble – folding the blade neatly in two so that she could test it twice as thoroughly, it was quite nice considering, and definitely eatable.

'If something *is* about to happen to me,' she decided, 'it may as well happen on a full stomach.'

Olga was extremely busy for the next few minutes. In no time at all she had cleared such a large patch in front of her she was almost up to the main building, and her mind was so at peace it was hard to believe it had ever been otherwise.

It was while breaking off for a well-earned rest that Olga suddenly had an odd feeling she was being watched. She looked round carefully, but apart from a few seagulls wheeling in the sky overhead there wasn't a soul in sight; and she'd just returned to her nibbling when she nearly jumped out of her skin with fright.

Just in front of her there was an opening in the wall of the main building which she hadn't noticed before, and standing barely a whisker's length away in the darkness beyond was another guinea-pig. It was so close, and it was staring back at her so unwinkingly, she might well have been looking at a reflection of herself in a mirror.

For a moment neither of them spoke, and then the other stirred.

'You must be Olga,' he said. 'I was told you were coming.'

Olga nodded, for her mouth was still too full to do anything else.

'You're not one of the Volga Olgas, are you, by any chance?'

Olga gobbled down the remains of the grass. 'One of the *Volga* Olgas?' she repeated, taken aback for the moment by this sudden and unexpected question. 'Most certainly *not*!'

'Pity.' The other guinea-pig made to leave and then paused. 'The Volga,' he said, looking back at Olga, 'happens to be a river in Russia. And if you'd been Russian I might have let you have a feed of my oats. As it is, I'm afraid I must ask you to leave by the next troika.' With that he turned on his heels and disappeared into the darkness.

Olga stared at the spot where he'd been for quite a while, trying to make up her mind about the matter. 'Volga?' she kept repeating to herself. ' *Troika*? What *can* he have been on about?

'Perhaps,' she thought, 'I was right after all. Perhaps there *are* some princesses being kept a prisoner. Guinea-pig princesses. Perhaps they have a mad father. Perhaps . . .'

And then she gathered herself together. 'Wheeee!'

25

she shrieked into the opening. 'This is a fine way to treat a sea-side guest. I wouldn't have any of your oats for all the groundsel in the world. I wouldn't . . .' She broke off as a figure appeared in the opening again.

'I'm sorry,' said the other guinea-pig. 'It was very rude of me. It was just that for one moment I thought perhaps . . .' A sad note crept into his voice, and then with an effort he pulled himself together. 'By the way, my name's Boris,' he continued, abruptly changing the subject. 'Boris Borski. Most people just call me Boris. I expect you saw it written above my hutch. This is my summer residence.'

Olga felt a pang of disappointment. She wasn't a new animal after all. 'Boris,' she repeated, putting on one of her superior expressions. 'That's very short.'

'I do have others,' said Boris grandly. 'But I won't bother you with them today. They're Russian and they all have *skis* on the end.' He gave a yawn. 'It's tiring having to go through the lot.'

'I have a *very* long name,' said Olga, not wishing to be outdone. 'And the Sawdust people said it's sort of Russian. It's *Olga da Polga*.'

'That's not *real* Russian,' said Boris scornfully. 'If it was *real* Russian it would have a *ski* on the end. It would be Olga da Polski. All Russians have a *ski* on the end of their names. At least, all the ones I saw last ni...' He broke off, as if he'd said something he hadn't meant to, and tried to cover his confusion by staring even more accusingly at Olga.

But Olga was hardly listening. While Boris was talking her mind had been racing on ahead.

'I *would* have had one,' she said, 'but it fell off when my ancestors were crossing the Alps. There were hundreds of them and it was bitterly cold at the time. It was so cold all the *skis* fell off the ends of their names and got left behind in the snow. That's why,' she continued wildly, remembering a conversation she'd once heard the Sawdust family having, 'even to this day they have places in the Alps called *ski resorts*. People go there from all over the world just to see where it happened. They've even tried using *ski lifts* to get them out, but it's no good . . .'

Olga's voice trailed away as she suddenly realized she was talking to herself.

Looking most offended, she stared at the opening. Really, she wasn't used to such treatment when she was telling one of her tales, particularly when she was just about to get into her stride.

'If you like,' Boris reappeared again as mysteriously as he'd left, 'I'll tell *you* a story.'

'*You* tell *me* a story!' Olga could hardly believe her ears, and for a brief moment her indignation was so great she was hard put to think of a suitable reply. Then gradually her curiosity got the better of her. After all, it *was* a nice day, and she *was* on holiday, and . . . 'If it gives you pleasure,' she said, not ungraciously.

'Mind you,' she added, as she settled herself down, 'it's quite possible I shall have heard it before. I know so many.'

'I doubt,' said Boris, 'if you've ever heard a story quite like this one. This story has been handed down!'

CHAPTER THREE

Boris's Story

'For this story,' said Boris, 'you will have to try and picture yourself living in Russia. This may not mean much to you, but my father used to be the Tzar. He ruled over the whole of the land. As far as the eye could see, from North to South, from East to West – it all belonged to him.'

Boris opened one eye cautiously in order to see how his tale was going so far. Olga returned his gaze with a mixture of surprise and admiration. She had to admit it was the kind of beginning she would have loved to have thought up herself.

'To look at me now,' said Boris, 'you probably wouldn't believe I was once a six-foot-three prince with blue blood in my veins.'

'I certainly wouldn't,' agreed Olga.

Boris looked slightly put out. 'Would you believe a *five*-foot-three prince with pink blood?' he asked.

'I might,' said Olga, not wishing to put him off completely in case she missed something exciting.

Boris settled back into himself. 'When I think about it,' he continued, before Olga had time to change her mind, 'it seems only yesterday that I used to sit on the steps outside my father's palace listening to the balaleikas. Afterwards we would all go for long rides through the snow on a horse-drawn sledge. I can still hear the sound of the bells tinkling in the moonlight. We had a real moon in those days. A great big one – not like that thing they've got up there now.'

He gave a sigh. 'All that was a long time ago, of course. Before I came down to this.'

Olga looked about her. 'It seems all right to me,' she said. 'I don't know any other guinea-pigs who have a castle all to themselves.'

'But it's not what I've been *used* to,' said Boris.

'That's the thing. Not even a hook for a chandelier – nothing. Once you're *used* to these things it's hard to make the change.'

'I was brought up in a pet shop,' said Olga. '*I* made the change all right.'

'A pet shop?' echoed Boris. He gave a hollow laugh. 'A *pet shop*? Do you realize that when I was small we had more servants than there are blades of grass in this run? I never had to lift a finger. I just *thought* what I wanted and it happened. My every wish was granted.'

'We were cleaned out every day,' said Olga. 'And we always had food. I don't see what else there is to think about.'

'I'll tell you what there was to think about,' said Boris grandly. 'Nothing! All day long there was nothing to think about – except having fun. And every evening, after dinner, there was a ball. People dressed up in their finest clothes and wore their most precious jewels, and we danced, and we sang, and we ate until we could eat no more.

'And next morning the troikas would draw up outside the palace gates carrying fresh supplies of grass from the near-by plains. Then it would begin all over again.'

'*Grass*?' repeated Olga suspiciously.

'In those days,' said Boris hurriedly, 'even humans

liked grass. Besides, it wasn't ordinary stuff. We had our own special fields, where the blades were as tall as a man and twice as thick as the arms of those who were sent out to gather it.'

Olga tried hard to picture the kind of grass Boris had just described compared with the sort Mr Sawdust brought in from the lawn each morning. 'If it was all so nice,' she said, giving it up as a bad job, 'what made you come and live here?'

'I'm very glad you asked me that,' said Boris, looking as if he felt quite the opposite.

'Well?' demanded Olga impatiently.

'You probably won't believe this next bit,' said Boris, 'but the people – the very same people my father had looked after all his life – they held a revolution and they all rose up and attacked the palace!'

'I don't find it a bit hard to believe,' said Olga bluntly. 'Not if you kept on telling them what a fine time you were having. I expect they wanted one too.' In point of fact Olga herself was beginning to tire of Boris's story with all its harping on the good things of life.

'That's all very well,' said Boris, 'but the thing is I was about to be married.' A dreamy look came into his eyes. 'My bride-to-be had light-blue eyes and hair the colour of ripening oats. She was said to be the most beautiful princess in all the land . . .'

'Story princesses always are,' said Olga knowledgeably. 'I've never ever heard of an ugly one.'

Boris chose to ignore the interruption. Instead he began running round and round in circles as he warmed to his tale.

'It was early morning when the first attack began, and it was all over within the hour. The guards held out as long as they could, but they were heavily outnumbered. Boom! Boom! Bang! Bang! Bang! One by one they fell at their posts, and gradually the mob got nearer and nearer, until at last they were inside the palace grounds and hammering on the door.'

He paused in mid-run and turned to Olga. 'What do you think my father did then?'

'I've no idea.' Olga tried hard to make it sound as if she didn't care either, but without much success. Although one half of her wasn't sure whether to believe Boris or not, the other half was only too eager to try. 'What *did* he do?'

'He sent for the Court Magician,' said Boris, 'and he ordered him to change us both into guinea-pigs. We were put into separate hutches in the Royal guinea-piggery for safety, and there we stayed.

'I expect you can guess the rest,' he said sadly. 'The Magician was supposed to change us back again when it was all over, but he was killed in the fighting, so there we were – stuck.

'After a day or two we were each set free at different times and went our separate ways. It's said that only if we both meet up again will we ever change back into our real selves. That's why, when I heard you were coming to stay, I thought perhaps . . .' Boris's voice trailed away and then with an effort he pulled himself together again. 'To think,' he said dramatically, 'all those diamonds and things in Russia really belong to me. Why, just one of them would probably keep me in oats for the rest of my life. But when you add up all the guinea-pigs there must be in the world . . .'

Olga looked at him thoughtfully. 'How will you know your princess when you meet her?' she asked.

Boris gazed back at her. 'I suppose,' he said carefully, 'you *could* ask the same thing of her.'

Olga took a deep breath and put on one of her far-away expressions. 'You know,' she said, 'I think *I* have a story coming on now. Shall we go over in the corner? You never know who might be listening, and it's really rather special.'

Olga had enjoyed Boris's tale, but more than that it

had set her own mind awhirl. Now she felt it was most definitely her turn.

When they had settled down again she began to talk. She talked and she talked and she talked; all through the morning and on into the afternoon as well. She talked so much neither of them even glanced at the grass all round them, let alone ate any; and when she had finished they lay for a long while basking silently together in the afternoon sun.

'Fancy,' said Boris at last, 'I've waited all this time.' He snuggled closer to Olga. 'And now you're here, my princess.'

'Now *we're* here,' said Olga pointedly. 'How nice it's going to be to share everything.'

Olga felt very pleased with herself, and she could tell that Boris was very impressed too. All the best story tellers believe in their own tales and by now Olga was convinced hers was true.

She wondered what it would be like living in Russia, and whether the Sawdust family would come and visit her. No doubt she would soon get used to all the servants.

They stayed for a while longer without saying anything, then she looked up at the sky. Goodness alone knew how long they had been together, for the sun was already sinking behind the far wall.

'I wonder how long it takes to change back into a princess?' she remarked dreamily. 'I hope the Sawdust people take me out of here first. There won't be room to stand and I don't want to get my golden locks caught in all that wire netting.'

But for some reason Boris had suddenly become restless. He didn't seem at all concerned about possible damage to Olga's hair.

He grew more and more impatient, and as the sun finally disappeared from view he jumped to his feet and hurried across to the front door.

'Is anything the matter?' asked Olga.

'They're late,' said Boris crossly. 'It's getting dark and they're late.'

Olga badly wanted to know who and how and why, but by then Boris was looking so worried she didn't dare ask for fear of upsetting him even more. In any case she didn't get the chance, for at that moment Karen Sawdust came down the garden path, and before she could utter so much as a goodbye 'Wheeeee!' Olga found herself back in her hutch.

Shortly afterwards the people they were staying with went past carrying Boris.

Olga called out, but Boris obviously had his mind on other things, for he either didn't hear, or if he did he couldn't be bothered to answer, and a moment later he'd disappeared into the big house along with the others.

When all was quiet again Olga peered at her reflection in the water. It had been a strange day. She felt quite different after it. Somehow, she had the feeling things would never be the same again. As for Boris . . . she gave a deep sigh . . . he was really rather handsome. A trifle gloomy perhaps – which, if all he'd said was true, wasn't surprising – but very handsome. The rosettes in his fur were quite the nicest she had ever seen – apart from her own, of course. Looking at him it was easy to believe he might once have been a prince. He would make a very suitable husband.

Stirring at last, Olga scrabbled about in her hay for a moment or two, fluffing it up to make it more comfortable. As she did so she wondered if it would be her last night in a hutch, and how she would take to the feel of silken sheets.

She'd seen sheets hanging on the line at the Sawdust family's house and she'd often wondered how anyone could possibly sleep in them. Perhaps she would soon find out.

When she'd finished making her bed Olga spent some time trying to make up her mind which way to lie. In the end she decided to sleep half in the dining-room, half in the bedroom, in order to leave plenty of room for expansion.

It would hardly do for a princess to begin her life

stuck inside a guinea-pig hutch and suffer the indignity of having to be sawn out.

Soon she was fast asleep.

CHAPTER FOUR

A Rude Awakening

In contrast to her first evening away from home, Olga didn't sleep at all well that night. She seemed to spend most of the time dreaming. If she wasn't listening to balalaikas she was riding through snow on horse-drawn sledges, or dancing or climbing in and out of troikas. When she woke she felt quite worn out by it all.

Worse still, for a second or two she had a job to move, and for a dreadful moment she thought she really had changed into a princess and was stuck inside the hutch. But it turned out she had somehow or other got her head stuck beneath an old ash branch Boris kept in a corner for his teeth.

Once free and properly awake she could hardly wait for the moment when they would be together again, especially when she heard Mr Sawdust say it was their last morning at the sea-side, and when at long last she was put in the outside run she hurried eagerly towards the tower in the far corner.

'Wheeeeeee!' she squeaked. 'Wheeeeeeeee! I'm here! Boris, I'm here!'

A familiar face appeared in the opening and regarded her without so much as a flicker of recognition.

'Morning all,' said Boris, in a polite but unusually gruff voice. 'What can I do for you?'

Olga stared back at him. This wasn't the kind of welcome she'd expected; if indeed it could be called a welcome at all.

Seeing that it was up to him to make the next move, Boris cleared his throat and made a sort of grunting noise. 'Er ... to look at me,' he said, 'you probably wouldn't think I was once a six-foot-two policeman.'

'A six-foot-two policeman?' echoed Olga, as if in a dream.

'In my cotton socks,' said Boris. 'I was a lot taller in my boots.'

He stared accusingly at Olga. 'Where were you on the twenty-ninth?' he demanded.

'Where was I on the twenty-ninth?' Once again Olga found herself repeating Boris's words, for the simple reason that for the life of her she couldn't think of anything else to say.

'You'd better have an answer by the time I get back,' said Boris sternly. 'Otherwise I may have to take down your particulars.'

'Take down my particulars!' wailed Olga. 'But I haven't got any particulars. I'm Olga da Polga. Your princess . . . remember?'

But Boris not only showed no sign of being aware of Olga's new position in life, he didn't even appear to remember a single thing that had taken place the previous day.

'If you like,' he said, 'I'll tell you a story. It's all about a detective. It's very exciting.'

Olga stared back at him open-mouthed. For once she was completely at a loss for words. Then she gave him a look. It was the most withering look she could manage. It was so withering it ought by rights to have gone straight through Boris and out through the concrete wall behind him as well, and it left her feeling quite weak.

'That's the last time I ever talk to anyone at the sea-side,' she announced to herself, as she turned her back. 'And it's certainly the very last time I let anyone tell me a story. Why, there wasn't an ounce of truth in it from start to finish. How anyone can tell stories like that I just don't know . . . I shall never believe anything anyone tells me again.'

In her indignation Olga hardly knew whether she was coming or going. All she wanted was to get back home again. Thank goodness it was her last morning away. She couldn't wait to leave. Even the grass had a nasty taste and kept getting stuck in her throat.

Altogether Olga was so upset by the outcome of her

week-end with Boris she hardly squeaked a word on the journey home and even the Sawdust family began to look worried.

'I do hope she hasn't had a relapse,' said Karen Sawdust. 'She was looking so well first thing this morning. Perhaps I shouldn't have put her out with Boris.'

'That,' thought Olga, 'is the first sensible thing I've heard said today!'

'Maybe,' said Mrs Sawdust, 'she's missing him. They seemed to be getting on terribly well together.'

'And *that*,' thought Olga, 'is so far from being the

second most sensible thing I've heard, it just isn't true. *Me* – miss *Boris*? Really! Humans haven't got much sense at times. I don't give a "Wheeee!" if I never set eyes on him again!'

And she let out such a cry of disgust at the very idea Mr Sawdust nearly lost control of the car and drove them all into a ditch.

On the other hand, although she kept thinking these things to her 'outer self', Olga had very different thoughts deep inside her. In spite of everything, her 'inner self' still couldn't help thinking about him, and when she heard his name mentioned she pricked up her ears at once.

'Funny chap, Boris,' said Mr Sawdust. 'Very independent. Probably comes from living in a castle.'

'More likely all that television,' said Mrs Sawdust. 'It can't be good for him. I've never seen an animal stay quite so glued to a screen before. He looked most upset yesterday evening when they turned it off before the programme finished.'

'It's the same every night apparently,' broke in Karen Sawdust. 'They have a job to get him away from it. He runs up and down in front of the set when it's a cowboy film, and he sits very still when it's a story. He really seems to take it all in. It must have an effect.'

'I suppose it's a bit like Olga was with the ballet that

time,' agreed Mrs Sawdust. 'After she'd had that fall. It wasn't until she saw *The Dance of the Sugar Plum Fairy* on the television that she began to get better.'

'Two of a kind really, I suppose,' said Mr Sawdust.

Olga sank back into her hay as the voices droned on.

So that was it. Television! That box with moving pictures the Sawdust people had in their home. Boris led a different life each day according to the kind of programme he'd seen the night before. One day a Russian prince, the next day a detective. She understood perfectly now.

Any disappointment Olga might have felt about not being a princess after all was more than made up for by knowing the truth of the matter. Goodness only knew what Boris would be tomorrow. She suddenly wished she was back with him so that she could find out.

If only she'd been more understanding. If only . . . but it was too late now. *Much* too late. Olga resolved there and then never to jump to conclusions again.

'Fancy us being two of a kind!' she squeaked. 'Wheeeeeeee! How exciting!'

Now that her mystery had been solved she was dying to get back home so that she could tell the others. Considering all the things that had happened to her she felt sure that she could make up a tale fanciful enough to impress even Noel the cat, let alone her other friends, Fangio and Graham.

CHAPTER FIVE

Olga Solves a Mystery

The rest of the journey seemed to take an age, but as soon as she was safely inside her house she rushed to the front door and called out in order to let the others know she was back.

A moment later Fangio and Graham, who'd obviously been hanging about inside the shrubbery, came out to greet her.

'You'll never guess where I've been,' squeaked Olga as they drew near. '*I've* been to the sea-side. *And* I

50

stayed with a prince! He was a detective prince, and there aren't many of those left!'

Olga had decided there was no need to tell the others *everything* about her week-end. Some stories were all the better for what was left out rather than what was put in.

But as it happened, before the others had a chance to reply, the back door of the big house opened and various members of the Sawdust family came outside and began shouting and whistling and calling for Noel.

Olga felt rather pleased, not only because she liked a big audience, but also because she'd been rushing

about so much she really needed time to compose herself. 'I may as well wait for him,' she said carelessly. 'I know he'll want to hear all about my adventures.'

'You'll be lucky,' said Fangio gloomily. 'I haven't seen him since the night you went away.'

'You've not seen him?' Olga felt her heart suddenly miss a beat.

'I haven't either,' agreed Graham. 'Not that *that* means anything of course. When you're a tortoise you can sometimes go for days without seeing anyone if you happen to be facing the wrong way.'

Olga looked from one to the other, hardly able to believe her ears. 'But he was left in charge of someone,' she wailed. 'He was left in charge of a neighbour. They were coming in to feed him and make sure he

was all right. I heard the Sawdust family talking about it.'

'Well, he's not there now by the sound of it,' said Graham bluntly. 'They wouldn't be out looking for him otherwise.'

Fangio nodded. 'If you want my opinion,' he said ominously, 'it means one thing, and one thing only. Noel's missing.'

'Perhaps,' suggested Fangio, as the Sawdust family went indoors again, 'he got on a lorry by mistake and was driven off. He could be anywhere by now.' Living as he did in a garage, Fangio was very motoring minded.

'He might even have been run over,' said Graham gloomily.

Fangio considered the matter for a while. 'It's

possible,' he said dubiously. 'Although I should have thought we'd have heard something if he has. Still, I'll make inquiries.'

Being used to death all around them, on the roads and in the woods and hedgerows, Graham and Fangio tended to look on Noel's disappearance as being part of the general pattern of things. They were sorry of course, but being sorry didn't change things and to-morrow would be another day, full of other problems to worry about.

'These things happen,' said Fangio comfortingly, as he caught sight of the look on Olga's face. 'It happens to us hedgehogs all the time. Take a simple thing like crossing a road. You look right, you look left, you look right again. And what happens? Whizz, bang, wallop . . . in between looking left and looking right something comes rushing up from behind and squashes you flat as a pancake. I tell you, you're much better off living in a hutch. You're not safe anywhere these days.'

'It's worse if you're a tortoise,' said Graham. 'If you live in a round shell like me and haven't even got a right or a left to start with you don't know where you are.'

The others digested this piece of information. Graham had a habit of coming out with odd statements from time to time, and they somehow felt there was a flaw in this particular one. But neither of them could put their paw on it and they were too unsure of their ground to argue, so soon afterwards the meeting broke up.

Olga sat where she was, staring into space. It was all right for Fangio and Graham; they were able to roam the countryside at will, wherever and whenever they wanted to. But she relied entirely on having visitors and the thought of never again seeing Noel made her sadder than she would have dreamed possible. The world suddenly seemed a colder place and for a long while she stared unblinkingly at the spot where she'd last seen him in the hope that he might reappear as if by magic.

Catlike, Noel often disappeared for hours on end. Sometimes for a whole day. But he always turned up again. No one knew where he went to on his rambles, and the only time Olga had ever questioned him he'd put on such a superior expression she'd decided never to give him the pleasure of hearing her ask again. Now she wished she had.

Noel had survived many adventures, but as the day wore on and there was still no sign of the familiar black shape wending its way slowly up the garden Olga grew more and more unhappy. What with chasing birds and investigating various crackles in the under-growth it sometimes took him ages to reach the house, but he'd never, ever, taken this long before.

The evening started to draw in, but still she didn't move. She refused to believe that anything had happened to him. She simply refused to believe it. She knew . . . she just knew, he must be somewhere around. The thing was . . . where? And how could she, shut inside her house, ever hope to find out?

For the umpteenth time Olga found herself wondering what Boris would have done. Boris, the detective, would have known what to do. Boris, the detective, would have looked for clues. Boris would have . . .

'Oh, Olga!' Karen Sawdust, her voice strangely subdued, appeared at the door. She opened it and held out her hands for Olga to climb into. 'I wish you could come in with us. But Daddy's lit the fire and he piled so much coal on before we left it's roaring away like nobody's business. Mummy thinks you'd get roasted alive and you wouldn't like that. Besides, I couldn't bear it if anything happened to you as well.'

She gave Olga her supper and then said goodnight before putting up the wooden front over the door to keep out the chilly night air.

When she was alone again Olga had a quick nibble of her oats and then wandered slowly and thoughtfully into her bedroom.

Something Karen had said was on the tip of her mind. What could it have been? She went over the conversation a dozen times. It had been mostly about fires and coal and being roasted, catching a cold . . . She tried turning the words about, sideways, back to front, every possible way . . . fire, coal, roasted, coal, roasted, fire, coal . . . And then, just as she was about to give up, she let out a squeak of excitement. 'Wheeeeeeeee!' It was there! It was there! Her first clue.

Her heart pounding away nineteen to the dozen, Olga turned her thoughts over in her mind several times. If Noel had been taken off on the back of a lorry then there was nothing she or anyone else could do about it, but if he *was* still somewhere around, then it was just possible . . . She came to a decision.

Hurrying across her room, she pressed her nose hard against the window and gave a loud squeak. 'Wheeeeeeee!' There was no reply. 'Wheeeeeee-eeeeee!' She tried again, louder this time, but still without success. Filling her lungs so full of air they felt as if they would burst at any moment, she gave one last, long, loud squeak. 'Wheeeeeeeeeeeeeeeeeeee!' It was really dark now. Dark and still, and the sound echoed eerily round the buildings before it disappeared into the night.

Olga lay back in her hay and listened, hardly daring to breathe for fear she might have been wasting her time. But sure enough, a moment later there came a faint answering meeow. It was a strange kind of meeow – a mixture of all kinds of things; relief, hope, frustration, bad-temper, impatience; but it definitely belonged to Noel, and in the circumstances it was the kind of meeow Olga would have expected him to make.

She closed her eyes, a look of quiet satisfaction on her face. Two clues in one evening was a very good start to being a detective. She felt even Boris would have been pleased with her efforts.

As for the rest; that would have to wait until morning. She had done all she could for the time being, and she would have a fine tale in the morning.

All about the clue she'd had the night before when Karen Sawdust had put her to bed . . . and the meeow in the night; plus a lot more things she'd made up, to do with tracks and pawprints. And of the long hours she'd had to wait until she'd been taken out for her daily run on the lawn. And how when she'd got near the outhouse she'd kicked up such a fuss Mr Sawdust had been forced to unlock the door and look inside . . .

*

'He's back! He's back! Noel's back!' Fangio, anxious to be first with the news, hurried up to Olga's outside run and peered through the wire netting.

'Is he really?' Olga pretended to sound rather bored by the news.

'He came back this morning,' chimed in Graham. 'Apparently he's been at a "meeow-in" all the time!'

Olga gave a start. 'A *what*?' she repeated.

'A meeow-in,' said Fangio knowledgeably. 'He's just been telling us all about it. It's something humans do all the time – only they call them "sit-ins" and "think-ins" and "teach-ins".'

'Noel's been holding one for all the cats in the district,' said Graham. 'It's like a "think-in" only instead of thinking they all sit in a circle and meeow. It's a wonder we didn't hear it.'

Olga stared at the others, a half-eaten blade of grass hanging from her mouth . . . 'I can tell you why you didn't hear anything,' she squeaked indignantly when she got her voice back. 'A *meeow-in* indeed! A "*shut-in*" more like it! Next time he tries to tell you that ask him why he smells of coal dust. You realize where he was? Locked in the coal cellar! He's been in there ever since I went away, only he's too ashamed to admit it. Of all the . . . why, if it hadn't been for me he would still be there . . . and serve him right . . .' Olga broke off. The others had gone.

'Cats!' she squeaked bitterly. 'Wheeeeeeeee! Of all the ungrateful, scheming, self-satisfied . . .' words failed her. 'I shall never, never, detect for one again!'

CHAPTER SIX

The Night of the Long Dance

'I suppose,' said Noel condescendingly, 'one advantage of having short legs is that when the weather's bad you can crawl under the nearest stone and keep dry.'

'I'd sooner do that,' replied Fangio, 'than get sopping wet every time it rains.'

'Who wants long legs anyway?' said Graham darkly. 'I don't. You sometimes see things you'd rather not. I stood on a mole-hill once and I didn't like what I saw at all. No wonder moles live underground.'

Olga chuckled to herself as she listened to the conversation going on to one side of her run.

The subject of legs had come up earlier that day when Fangio happened to pass a remark about the way Noel walked. Noel was a particularly beautiful cat. He was much given to taking up poses – draping himself on tree stumps or tops of walls in order to show off to the best advantage – but he was proudest of all about the way he walked, and Fangio's comment had set him going.

Although Noel secretly liked to be noticed he was a little upset by the fact that he had been, and he spent some time listing the countless advantages enjoyed by those who were lucky enough to have long legs, and the many, many drawbacks suffered by those who only had short ones.

Olga chuckled again as she basked in the afternoon sun. Although she still hadn't forgiven Noel over the episode with the coal shed, she had to admit that when he was on form he could be quite amusing in his superior kind of way.

Noel's voice suddenly broke into her daydreams. 'And what's *your* excuse?' he said.

Olga gave a start and looked around the garden. She hadn't realized they had been joined by someone else and she wondered who it could possibly be.

'Well?' Noel put his face against the wire.

Olga stared at him. 'Are you addressing me?' she asked coldly.

'Your legs are so short,' said Noel, 'I can't even see them.'

Slowly and carefully Olga drew herself up to her full height until she was practically standing on tip-toe. 'I keep them tucked under me for safety,' she said. 'Besides, I happen to have unusually long fur.'

'I suppose being so short has its uses,' said Noel, turning back to the others. 'I mean, it keeps the place tidy. You can sweep up as you go along.'

Fangio made a noise which sounded suspiciously

like a giggle, but it was quickly suppressed when he saw the look in Olga's eye.

'I admit,' Olga sank to the ground, because try as she might she couldn't hold her pose a moment longer, 'I admit that my legs could perhaps do with being a trifle longer – *if* I wanted to go around on stilts. But at least we guinea-pigs know what it's like to have long legs. We haven't always been like this. We guinea-pigs used to have the most beautiful legs imaginable. Long and slender and . . .'

'When was that?' demanded Noel. 'I've never seen a guinea-pig with long legs.'

'Oh, it was a long time ago,' said Olga vaguely. She picked on the thought that happened to be uppermost in her mind. 'It was in Russia.'

'Russia?' repeated Noel. 'Guinea-pigs don't come from Russia.'

'We may not *come* from there,' said Olga, 'but we've *been* there. You'll find guinea-pigs wherever they value breeding and good looks and . . .'

'Oh, *do* get on with it,' exclaimed Noel impatiently. In truth he was feeling a little put out that his afternoon's entertainment at the expense of Fangio and Graham had been interrupted.

Olga took a deep breath. 'For this story,' she said, taking a leaf out of Boris's book, 'you will have to try and picture yourself living in Russia at the time of the revolution.

'In those days the Tzar kept hundreds of guinea-pigs for his special pleasure, and they were said to have

the longest and most beautiful legs of any animal in the world.

'For a long time,' she added as an afterthought, 'they did try to breed some cats with legs half as long, but they never quite succeeded. Something always seemed to go wrong. They either bent the wrong way at the knees or else they fell off . . .'

Noel gave a loud snort.

'After the revolution,' continued Olga hurriedly, 'the people who had taken over the palace didn't know quite what to do to pass the time. They weren't used to the life, you see, and they soon got fed up with listening to ballylaikas all day . . .'

'Don't you mean *bala*laikas?' asked Noel suspiciously. Routing around in dustbins as he did Noel was apt to know about these things.

'If you'd had to listen to them all day long you'd have called them *bally*laikas too,' said Olga.

'Anyway, at last, when they could stand it no longer, their leader called on the Royal guinea-pigs to entertain them.

'At first the guinea-pigs didn't know what to do. Usually it was *they* who were entertained and not the other way round. But like guinea-pigs the world over, they were very gifted. The problem really was to decide which of their many talents would be most suitable.

'And then the sound of the music gave them an idea. Having such long and beautiful legs they were particularly good dancers, so that's what they did. They danced. Not the kind of dancing we know today, but special Russian dancing. They stood on their hind legs and they folded their front paws across their chests and away they went.

'The audience had never seen anything like it.

'"Moreski!" they cried. "Moreski! Moreski!"'

'And the louder they called out the faster the musicians played; and the faster the musicians played the faster the guinea-pigs had to dance. On and on it went. On into the night – hour after hour.'

'Show us some,' broke in Fangio.

Olga gave him a long, hard look. Really, she wondered for a moment whose side he was on – hers or Noel's. 'I will,' she said at last, 'after that aeroplane has passed over. It really is most distracting.'

'What aeroplane?' asked Noel.

'The one behind you,' said Olga.

Olga's audience turned and looked up at the sky.

'I can't see any aeroplanes,' said Noel, as they turned back again.

'It was going very fast,' said Olga. 'It was going almost as fast as the dance I just did for you.'

The others stared back at her in disbelief.

'Well, now the acroplane *has* gone,' said Noel, 'perhaps you can do it for us again.'

'It's a bit difficult on grass,' replied Olga, playing for time.

'There's a bare patch right behind you,' said Graham.

Olga suddenly gave a quick shuffle. 'Tarrraaaaaaa!' she exclaimed as a small cloud of dust rose into the air.

'Was that it?' demanded Noel scornfully.

'I didn't see a thing,' said Fangio.

'Nor me,' agreed Graham.

Olga gave a deep, deep sigh. 'Russian dancing is very quick,' she said. 'If you *will* look the other way or blink every time I'm afraid you'll never see it.

'Now,' she said wearily, 'I *must* get on with my story. Really, all this dancing has quite worn me out.

'Dawn,' she continued, 'was beginning to break when gradually the audience in the Tzar's palace noticed a very strange thing. In the beginning they'd been able to look out from their seats straight at the dancers; now they were looking down on them.

'The guinea-pigs,' said Olga dramatically, 'had danced so much they'd worn out their legs – right down to the ground.

'And that's why, to this very day, guinea-pigs – although they have very beautiful legs, also have rather short ones.'

The others fell silent for a moment or two, and Olga took the opportunity to go back to enjoying the sunshine, closing her eyes and snuggling down into the warm grass.

'Look,' Noel banged on the side of her run with his tail, 'if they stood on their back legs like you said, and danced them away, why haven't guinea-pigs got great big front ones still?'

'Here! Here!' echoed Fangio and Graham.

Olga opened one eye and put on her pained expression. There were some questions she just didn't choose to answer.

'If you don't mind,' she said, 'I happen to be fast asleep.'

CHAPTER SEVEN

Olga Takes the Plunge

One Saturday, soon after the week-end at the sea-side, Mr Sawdust set to work on the garden and began digging a hole. The animals watched with interest from a safe distance, for at first they weren't at all sure what he was up to. Clearly it was going to be a large hole, and equally clearly Mr Sawdust intended leaving it there, for he carted all the earth away in a wheel-barrow and dumped it at the bottom of the garden.

Graham, the tortoise, was particularly upset by it all. 'This garden's big enough as it is,' he grumbled. 'Fancy making a hole *that* size. If I go round it I shall have to walk twice as far, and if I go down inside I may never get out again.'

But the next day all was revealed. Olga had barely finished breakfast when Mr Sawdust staggered past her house bent almost double beneath the weight of what looked like an enormous grey bath. She was so taken aback she sat where she was with her mouth wide open trying to take it all in.

After Mr Sawdust had turned the bath on its back, he placed it carefully into the hole and then began mixing a lot of sand and water and grey powder stuff together, which he then poured between the bath and the sides of the hole.

Whatever it was he'd been doing he seemed very pleased with the result, for when he stood up again he called out for the others to come and see.

Olga thought perhaps he'd been building a water bowl for some enormous new pet the Sawdust family were getting, but Noel soon scotched that idea.

'It's not a water bowl,' he said scornfully. 'It's a pond. I know lots of houses where they've got one. You wait; in a few days' time they'll be putting fish and pots of plants in it. I know a pond when I see one.'

Noel was right, and as it began to take shape even Olga had to admit that Mr Sawdust's pond was really rather a splendid affair. It was built into the side of some sloping ground, and over the next few days he added three more smaller pools, each higher than the one before and overhanging it slightly, so that the whole formed one long waterfall.

After he had surrounded the pools with paving stones, Mr Sawdust spent some time connecting a thing called 'a pump', and there was great excitement one evening when he set it all in motion and water began cascading down from the topmost pool to the bottom.

Olga decided she liked Mr Sawdust's pond. It was near the spot on the lawn where she usually had her outside run and she found the sound of running water very soothing, especially on warm afternoons. But she enjoyed it just as much in the evenings, when all was still and the only sound was the soft plop-plopping of the fish as they surfaced in search of insects.

However, as with most things, everyone soon began to take Mr Sawdust's pool for granted and after a while it became so much a part of the normal scenery Olga almost forgot what the garden had been like without it.

It wasn't until a couple of weeks later that she was reminded of it in no uncertain manner.

She was enjoying a quiet nibble on the lawn when

all of a sudden she heard a tremendous scurrying in the near-by bushes. There followed a whirr of flapping wings and a moment later a bird – Olga was much too startled to take note of what sort – but it was definitely a bird, flew past her run with barely an inch to spare. It was hotly pursued by a black shape she had no trouble at all in recognizing.

It was Noel, and whether he was so intent on the task in hand he didn't see the pond, or whether in the excitement he'd forgotten all about it, or whether he thought he could clear the water in one bound, Olga didn't know. The fact remained that Noel didn't make it. He hurled himself into space, lost speed somewhere near the centre, hovered in mid-air for a fraction of a second, and then landed with a loud splash just short of the far side. Wild-eyed, he clawed des-

perately at the slippery edge for what seemed like an age, and then slowly sank back into the water, where he floundered around looking for a suitable paw-hold.

'Very good,' said Olga, when he finally managed to scramble out. 'What a bit of luck it wasn't any deeper. You might have drowned.'

Noel paused and gave her a look as he shook himself dry. 'If it had been you,' he said witheringly, '*that* would have been that!'

Olga bristled. 'Are you suggesting,' she exclaimed, 'that guinea-pigs can't swim?'

'No more than hedgehogs can fly,' snorted Noel, as he hurried up the garden towards the house.

'I'll have you know,' called Olga indignantly, 'that guinea-pigs happen to be very good swimmers. They're noted for it!' She peered through her wire at the pool. 'Why, two or three powerful strokes and I'd be at the other side and back while you were still thinking about it.'

But Noel didn't stop to argue. He disappeared through his pussy flap and there was a bang as it fell shut behind him.

A few seconds later there was another loud commotion and he came flying out again. It had something to do with wet paws and the fact that the kitchen floor had just been scrubbed, but whatever the reason Noel was obviously in an even worse mood than before as he came stalking down the garden.

'Two or three powerful strokes indeed!' he snorted as he reached Olga's run. 'Why, with legs like yours it'd be more like two or three hundred. Or two or three thousand. Or two or three . . .' Noel broke off, unable to think of any more figures.

Olga gave a sigh. 'What a pity I'm stuck here inside this run,' she said. 'If only I *could* show you. If only I was outside I'd jump in. If only . . .'

A wicked gleam came into Noel's eyes. He looked over his shoulder and then around the garden to make sure no one was watching, and then he sidled up to Olga's run and leant against it.

'What are you doing?' squeaked Olga nervously. As the bottom rose into the air she ran towards the boarded-up section at the back and scrabbled around anxiously. 'Wheeeeee! Watch out! You'll have me over if you're not careful.'

'Hurry up,' gasped Noel. 'I can't stay like this all day.'

'But I couldn't,' cried Olga. 'I really couldn't. I mean, *they* wouldn't like it.'

'*They* aren't watching,' said Noel. 'Come on, before I tip you right over.'

Olga hurriedly squeezed herself out beneath the side and watched forlornly while Noel lowered her run again.

'I really ought not to be doing this,' she said, clutching at straws. 'I've been very ill. That's why I was taken to the sea-side. I'm not at all well, really I'm not ...'

'I'm waiting,' said Noel menacingly.

Olga looked at his expression and then at the water. Of the two she infinitely preferred the latter. The pond had a placid look about it which was entirely absent from Noel's face.

'I won't do my best strokes to start with,' she said, peering over the edge. 'I may just play around for a while until I get used to the feel of the water.'

'In!'

Olga gave a gulp as Noel advanced towards her. There was something about the way his tail was brush-

ing to and fro on the ground she didn't care for at all.

Taking a deep breath she closed her eyes and slid gently forward on her stomach. The next moment she felt herself falling, and an icy shock as the water closed over her.

'Wheeeeeee!' she shrieked as she rose to the surface. The pool was twice as deep as she had expected, and the sides suddenly seemed an impossible distance away.

'Wheeeeeeee! Help! I can't touch the bottom!' How anyone could possibly swim in a pool where they couldn't touch the bottom Olga didn't know. Nor, for that matter, did she greatly care. All she wanted was to get out of it and on to dry land again. But the more she struggled the worse her plight became. She felt herself going round and round in circles. First Noel came into view, then the house in the far distance, then her run, then Noel again.

'Wheeeeeee!' She gave another despairing shriek as she felt herself sinking for the second time. In vain she clutched at a near-by lily, but it came away in her paw and everything went black.

How long it all lasted Olga never knew. It felt like a lifetime, and she'd long since given up all hope of ever being rescued when she felt a familiar pair of hands close around her.

She had never been so thankful in the whole of her life.

'Olga!' Karen Sawdust lifted her, dripping and bedraggled, from the pool. 'Olga, what *have* you been

doing? And how on earth did you ever get out of your run?'

Olga lay panting, struggling to get her breath back, utterly unable to give even the faintest of squeaks in reply.

Karen Sawdust looked at Olga's run and then at Noel. There was something about the way he was avoiding her gaze that struck her as highly suspicious.

'Noel!' she exclaimed. 'You naughty cat! Have you got anything to do with this?'

But Noel didn't reply either, and for an equally good reason. He was no longer there.

Gathering Olga in her arms, Karen Sawdust hurried indoors and ran up the stairs to the bathroom.

'You poor thing,' she said, as she wrapped Olga in a large and fluffy towel. 'Why, you might have drowned.' She held her up to a round mirror which stuck out from the wall on a long arm. 'Just look at you. Have you ever seen anything like it?'

Olga stared at herself. Karen Sawdust was right.

She did look a mess. Her fur was matted and stuck up in spikey tufts all over her head. Even her whiskers seemed to be sticking out at a funny angle.

Although it wasn't the first time she'd been shown her reflection, Olga had never been quite so close to herself before. She began to wish she looked better for the occasion. It really was the biggest 'her' she had ever seen.

'Never mind,' said Karen Sawdust. 'We'll soon have you back to normal.' And with that she pushed the mirror to one side and began rubbing the towel briskly up and down.

Olga felt a pleasant warm glow enter her body. It started somewhere near the middle and gradually made its way through the rest of her until even her toes began to feel as warm as toast.

She was just thinking to herself that perhaps swimming wasn't quite such a bad thing after all, when she suddenly let out a gasp of alarm.

'Wheeeeee! Wheeeeeeeeee!' she shrieked. 'Wheeeeeeeee!'

Karen Sawdust stopped rubbing and looked down at her with concern. 'What's the matter, Olga?' she asked. 'What's wrong?'

But Olga was much too busy looking at her reflection in the mirror to hear.

'I've shrunk!' she wailed. 'Wheeeeee! Wheeee! Wheeeeeee! I've shrunk!'

And it really did seem as though she had, for whereas when she'd first seen her reflection it had filled the whole of the glass, now it barely covered a quarter of it.

Olga sank back into Karen Sawdust's hands. 'It's the water,' she moaned. 'It's the water. I knew I shouldn't have gone swimming. Now I've dried out and I've shrunk!'

CHAPTER EIGHT

Olga Gets Her Own Back

Karen Sawdust held Olga up to the mirror with one hand and with the other she twisted the glass round until it faced the other way.

'Is that any better?' she asked.

Olga sat up and stared at her reflection in amazement. Not only was it better, but she had actually changed back into her old size again. Or rather, into the extra-big size she'd seen earlier on, for now that she looked at herself more closely she realized it was very much larger than life.

'It's Daddy's special shaving mirror,' explained

Karen Sawdust. 'One side is just like an ordinary mirror – see,' she turned the glass round and Olga suddenly became smaller again, 'the other side makes you look much larger. That's so that you can see your whiskers properly when you shave them off.'

It took Olga some while to absorb this strange piece of information; partly because she couldn't picture anyone in their right senses actually wanting to shave their whiskers off, and partly because she found the whole effect so exciting she couldn't draw herself away.

'You had me worried for a moment,' said Karen Sawdust. 'The way you were behaving I really thought I'd done something awful to you. Though if you ask me, I think I've come off worst.'

Sucking one of her thumbs, she examined Olga's paws and then looked her straight in the eye. 'Your toe-nails need cutting!' she announced.

'Now, you can either go to the Vet, or you can sit here quietly and let me do it. I promise I won't hurt, and it's quite safe as long as I only cut off the dead bits at the end – you can tell by the colour. But if they aren't done soon your nails will just carry on growing and bend right round until they dig back into the skin. You won't like that at all.'

It didn't take Olga very long to decide that although having her toe-nails grow back into her didn't sound very nice, having them cut was ten times worse, especially as the first choice had to do with something that was very much in the future, whereas the second choice was happening to her there and then.

'Why, oh why, can't toe-nails grow shorter instead of longer?' she moaned. 'It would save so much trouble. Wheeeeeeee!'

'Really!' exclaimed Karen Sawdust, 'no wonder they call you "Restless Cavies" in my book about guinea-pigs . . .'

Olga stopped struggling for a moment and pricked up her ears. 'A book?' she thought. 'About guinea-pigs?'

Olga knew all about books. The Sawdust people had lots. Rows and rows of them. And once, when she'd been left all by herself in their front room while her own house was being cleaned out, she'd actually had a nibble at one or two. And very good they'd been – just the thing for keeping teeth nice and trim. But she hadn't realized there was one all about her.

'Mind you,' she thought, 'I'm not surprised. It's probably very popular.'

Olga was so taken up by the thought of books that she almost forgot to squeak while the rest of her nails were being cut, and she looked very thoughtful indeed as she was being carried back downstairs to her run.

When she was settled in Karen Sawdust put a large
rockery stone on top of it for safety. 'There,' she
said, 'that won't get pushed over in a hurry.'

But Olga was much too busy with her thoughts to
answer. In fact, she was so quiet for the rest of that
morning that Noel began to look concerned.

'Are you all right?' he asked, peering through the
wire at her. 'I haven't heard a weeeeeek out of you
since you fell in the pond.'

Olga gazed up at him with a faraway look in her
eyes. 'I'm busy,' she said carelessly, running her paw
round a patch of dry earth to form a vague letter.
'I'm ... er ... I'm writing a book.'

'A book?' Noel looked at her in disbelief. '*You* . . . write a *book*? Guinea-pigs can't write books.'

'Guinea-pigs,' said Olga stiffly, 'can do most things. We can do things you cats haven't even dreamed of.' And she turned her back on him to show the conversation was at an end.

But the trouble was, although she knew she *could* write a book if she tried, she hadn't got an idea yet. It really needed peace and quiet, and these were two items she obviously wasn't going to get that day, for having disappeared into the undergrowth, Noel returned shortly afterwards followed by Fangio and Graham – both eager for news of the latest happening.

'Have you finished it yet?' called Fangio. 'Is it true it's all about swimming?'

'Wait for me,' cried Graham, as he hurried along behind. 'Don't start without me.'

Noél jumped on top of Olga's run and peered down

at her. 'Don't worry,' he called. 'There's no hurry.
I think she's run out of weeeeeeks. She used them all up
in the pond this morning. You should have heard the
noise . . .'

Olga grew more and more restive as Noel's voice
droned on. Really, just lately he'd been getting very
much above himself. It was about time he was taken
down a peg or two. The way he kept on about her
swimming anyone would think he was the world's
best. Just because his whiskers had dried out he'd
forgotten what a sight he'd looked. It was a good job
he hadn't seen himself in the bathroom mirror. It
would have turned them white. It would have . . .
Olga paused for a moment as an idea entered her mind.

'If you like,' she said, taking the plunge, 'I'll start
my book now. I haven't actually *written* it yet, but I
can tell you what it's about.'

Olga waited for a moment or two, partly to allow
her audience time to settle down, and partly to get her
own thoughts straightened out.

'This story,' she began, when all was quiet, 'took
place one fine summer's day in autumn.'

'I don't believe that for a start,' broke in Noel. 'You
can't have a fine summer's day in autumn. It doesn't
make sense.'

Olga gave him a look. 'Spring,' she said, 'had been a

little late that year. It was late because everything was the wrong way round. The world woke up one morning and found that left had become right, up had become down, black was white, and mornings were evenings.'

She lowered her voice. 'But something much, much worse had happened. Can you guess what?'

The others sat in silence for a moment or two trying to think of the worst possible thing that could happen.

'The fish man took the fish away instead of leaving it?' hazarded Noel.

Olga clicked her tongue impatiently. 'Food!' she exclaimed, taking a quick nibble at the grass. 'That's all some animals ever think about.

'No, I'll tell you. Things started to grow the wrong way. Grass gradually got shorter and shorter, trees turned into bushes, toe-nails got smaller.

'At first everyone thought it was great fun, but then they discovered they were getting smaller too. Instead of growing older they were getting younger every day. And that, too, seemed fun for a while, because nobody really likes growing old. But when they found they were beginning to forget all the things they'd ever learnt – even how to talk, they began to get really worried.

'The world was suddenly full of babies – and there was no one left to look after them.'

The others gave a shiver as they tried to picture the scene. 'I don't want to grow young,' moaned Graham. 'I want to stay as I am. I'm too old to die.'

'It won't happen, will it?' asked Fangio anxiously. 'I mean, it *is* only a story.'

'Perhaps,' said Olga cautiously, 'and perhaps not.'

She glanced across at Noel, who was sitting in a patch of noon-day sun. 'I haven't liked to say anything until now, but it has struck me you've not been looking quite so fat lately.'

Noel sat up. 'What do you mean?' he blustered.

'Have you noticed your shadow?' asked Olga. 'It's really very short. They do say that's the first thing to go when things start getting smaller. Shadows first – whiskers and fur last of all. I daresay yours will start dragging on the ground any day now. If I were you I'd make the most of things while you can.'

'But it's going to take me longer than ever to get anywhere,' wailed Graham.

'Cheer up,' said Olga. 'Think of all the things you'll be able to do when you get there. Things you've never done before.'

'Such as?' demanded Noel, who was beginning to believe the story in spite of himself.

'Go through gaps for a start,' said Olga. 'You won't have to rely on the width of your whiskers to see if you can get through or not.' She fixed him with a beady eye. 'Why, I bet there are gaps in that fence over there you could sail through already. Gaps you haven't been able to get through in years.'

'Go on,' exclaimed Fangio eagerly. 'Have a go!'

'Quick, before it's too late!' cried Graham.

'I don't want to,' said Noel.

'Coward!' said Olga accusingly.

Noel gave her a long, hard look, and then he turned on his heels and stalked off without so much as a backward glance.

'Do you think he will?' asked Fangio.

'Will what?' asked Olga innocently, as she turned to examine a particularly succulent-looking dandelion.

'Have a go,' said Fangio.

'Get through the gap,' chorused Graham.

Olga considered the matter, but before she had time to reply there was a long-drawn-out yowl from somewhere near by.

'I think,' she said, when the noise had died down, 'the answer is "yes", and then again "no".'

Noel's yowl had had a particular quality about it which she found very rewarding. It was a yowl of surprise and indignation rather than of pain, and it more than made up for the indignities she'd suffered earlier in the day.

Olga took a long nibble from her dandelion. All in all, she felt it was a most satisfying note on which to end a story.

CHAPTER NINE

Olga to the Rescue

One evening, a week or so later, Olga had a strange experience.

She was sitting quietly in her hutch enjoying the last of the day, when she heard an unusual noise. It had a kind of rasping note and every now and then it was punctuated by a loud smack.

Oddly enough, although she could tell that it came from somewhere near the Sawdust family's kitchen she couldn't for the life of her see what was causing it.

There was a glass panel in the door and when the light was on, as it happened to be that evening, Olga could often see shadows flittering back and forth.

The shadows and the clinking sounds that usually accompanied them were very comforting and she was always sorry when they stopped.

But the present noises had nothing to do with the Sawdust family, for they were most definitely coming from somewhere *outside* the kitchen, not within.

As Olga turned the matter over in her mind she gradually became aware of another very odd thing. Usually when the light was on it attracted insects – flies, gnats, moths; all kinds of annoying creatures she could have well done without. But for once they seemed few in number, and they were getting fewer all the time.

It was while she was idly following the progress of one of these denizens of the night that Olga solved her mystery.

As the insect swooped low past the bottom of the door a large greeny-yellow creature with bulbous eyes and an enormous mouth to match suddenly rose up out of the darkness. There was a snap and in one swift movement victor and victim disappeared from view as the former sank down on to its haunches and merged once again with the shadows.

Olga's eyes nearly popped out. It was all over before she'd had time to say 'sliced carrots' once over forwards, let alone twice over backwards.

She was about to let out a warning squeak for the benefit of anyone else who might be around when the kitchen door opened and Mr Sawdust came into view carrying a pile of rubbish.

'Thank goodness for that!' breathed Olga, as he crossed in front of her on his way to the dustbin. 'Now perhaps it'll go away – whatever it is.'

Brief though her glimpse had been, she had no wish to see the creature again. It was quite the ugliest she had ever come across. In fact she was just wondering whether or not she ought to warn Mr Sawdust himself when she suddenly realized he was talking to someone. Someone or some*thing*.

'Hullo, old chap,' he was saying.

Olga gave a start. Don't say he was actually speaking to the object? She could hardly believe her ears.

But it was true. In fact, not only was Mr Sawdust talking to it; he was even inviting others to do the same.

'I say,' he called. 'We've got a visitor. Do come and have a look.'

Mrs Sawdust appeared in the doorway. 'Ugh!' she exclaimed. 'I knew something like this would happen. It's that wretched pond of yours.'

Olga nodded approvingly. At least she had someone on her side.

Mr Sawdust stood up. '*My* wretched pond?' he repeated indignantly. 'I like that!

'Anyway,' he continued stoutly, 'I'm rather fond of toads. They've lots of character.' He bent down again. 'I must say he's quite a specimen and he looks very venerable. I bet he's twenty years old if he's a day. I wonder what he's doing here?'

'Probably after the insects,' said Karen Sawdust, joining the group. 'It's because we have a glass door. The light attracts them, and toads like insects. I expect he'll be coming here every night for his supper from now on.'

'In that case,' said Mr Sawdust, 'we'd better leave him to enjoy it. We don't want to give him indigestion.'

The voices died away as the Sawdust family went back indoors. It seemed that the toad had also decided it was time to leave – either because he'd been frightened or because he felt sufficiently full for one night, for there was a swish and a plop as he went past Olga's house, then another swish and a plop and he was gone.

In spite of everything Olga couldn't help admiring the way he moved. The sudden leap into space without any warning whatsoever, and the absolute stillness that followed.

Carefully making sure no one else was watching she tried a few practice leaps herself, but the most she could manage was a couple of inches and even then she ended up by banging her head against the side of her hutch.

Of course, having so much space must give toads a tremendous advantage, and ugly though they were, large eyes must be quite a help. You could see things before they actually hit you.

All the same, she felt most impressed.

Olga was very quiet the next day. Truth to tell she was looking forward to seeing her new friend again, and remembering Mr Sawdust's words she decided she would call him Venerables.

She tried out the word several times and decided she liked it. It had a nice 'old' sound to it that went very well with a toad.

Olga waited impatiently for night to fall. It had been a hot, cloudless day, and the sun took an age to disappear behind the trees at the bottom of the garden. Normally Olga was rather sad to see it go, but tonight she just couldn't wait.

As the gnats and the midges began to beat against the kitchen door she almost gave up hope, when suddenly there was a familiar swish and a plop and a snap and it was just as it had been the night before.

Olga peered through her wire netting. 'Good evening, Venables,' she called. Somehow, although she knew this time she hadn't got the word quite right, she felt it sounded even better.

'Venables!' she called, trying it out again. 'Wheeee-eeeeee! Venables!'

There was no reply. Venables was either too busy or too intent on his supper to answer.

'I've decided to call you Venables,' said Olga, 'because I think it suits you very well. Everyone should have a name. Being a toad, I don't suppose you've ever thought about it, but if you've a name it will make you different from all the other toads, and that could be very useful . . .'

Olga paused for a moment as a sudden thought struck her. 'You *are* the same toad who came last night?' she asked.

Faintly through the darkness there came an answering croak, though whether or not it was in reply to her question Olga never did find out, for just then the kitchen door opened.

'He's here again,' said Karen Sawdust excitedly. 'I told you he would be.'

'Leave him be,' called Mrs Sawdust. 'Dinner's almost ready and we don't want him leaping about the kitchen.'

From somewhere inside the house Olga heard Mr Sawdust give an answering laugh. 'Might be rather apt,' he said. 'All things considered.'

And then he made a remark that sent a cold shiver running down Olga's spine. It was so unlike anything she had ever heard him say before that really, she wondered if she had heard aright. But Karen Sawdust's next words confirmed her worst fears.

'Oh, Daddy!' she exclaimed. 'What an awful thought. How could you?'

As the door closed again Olga peered out of her hutch, her mind in a turmoil. Why on earth didn't Venables make a run for it – or hop for it – or whatever toads did when their lives were in danger?

'Wheeeeeeee!' she shrieked. 'Wheeeeeeeeeeee! Wheeeeeeeeeee!'

But it was no good. No matter how hard she shrieked, Venables either couldn't or didn't want to hear, and gradually it was borne on her mind that perhaps he couldn't understand what she was saying anyway.

It wasn't long before her cries brought Fangio and Graham hurrying onto the scene. They were closely followed by Noel.

'It's Venables!' shrieked Olga. 'You *must* warn Venables! Do something. For goodness sake *do* something!'

'Do calm down,' said Noel, stifling a yawn. 'Anyone would think you were being murdered.'

'Venables may be if you don't hurry,' gasped Olga.

'Venables?' repeated Fangio. 'Who's *Venables*?'

'Venables,' said Olga, when at last she'd managed to get her breath back, 'is a very close toad friend of mine who happens to be in great danger. Very great danger indeed. In fact,' she lowered her voice, '*he's about to be eaten by the Sawdust people.*'

'A toad?' said Graham. 'Fancy anyone wanting to
eat a toad. Mind you, humans do funny things.'
He turned to Fangio. 'I have heard they're very keen
on hedgehogs. They wrap them in clay and bake them.
Then, after a couple of hours good roasting they
break open the clay and all the prickles come away.'

Fangio took this piece of information with a

distinct lack of enthusiasm. 'Where is this friend of yours?' he asked, hurriedly changing the subject.

'Right behind you,' said Olga. 'At least, he was just now. Venables! Venables! Wheeeeee! Are you there, Venables?'

The answering croak made even Noel jump. He examined the cause of it dubiously. All his instincts called for him to reach out a paw and administer a pat if only to see what happened, but he stopped short at the sound of Olga's voice.

'We *must* stick together,' she said. 'We *must* make Venables a hideaway.'

'*We?*' Fangio looked up at her suspiciously.

'I shall be here to direct you,' said Olga grandly. 'And I shall keep watch in case the Sawdust people come.'

'Sometimes,' murmured Graham, 'I wish I lived in a hutch.'

'You're very welcome to climb up and open my front door,' said Olga, whose sharp ears missed nothing. 'I shall be only too pleased to help.'

Faced with this impossible task the others had no choice but to give in.

Noel took one last hopeful look at Venables and then made his way towards the shrubbery. 'Come on,' he called grumpily. 'Let's get to work. I'll do the digging. You can fetch the leaves and things.'

For some time the only sound to reach Olga's ears was the soft scratching of earth and the occasional snapping of a twig as the others busied themselves in the undergrowth.

It all took much longer than expected and the moon was high in the sky by the time the job was done. As the others limped wearily into view Olga had to admit to herself that she wasn't altogether sorry she'd been unable to join in, for they were so covered in dirt and leaves they were barely recognizable. Noel's fur in particular looked as if another dip in the pool wouldn't come amiss.

'I hope you're satisfied,' he gasped, as they drew near her hutch.

'They won't find him in that hole in a hurry,' said Fangio.

'A hole?' echoed Olga. 'A hole? Don't say you've put Venables down a *hole*?'

The others looked at her. 'What's wrong with that?' demanded Noel.

'But that's what the Sawdust family were going to do!' wailed Olga. 'I heard Mr Sawdust say so. He said "What a bit of luck Venables was outside the kitchen door because that was what they were having for supper – Toad in the Hole." Karen Sawdust was very upset.'

Olga broke off and peered out at Noel. For some reason or other he appeared to be having a kind of fit. He really was behaving most strangely. Unless her eyes were deceiving her he was almost foaming at the mouth, and some of his meeows were quite blood-curdling.

'Toad in the Hole!' he said bitterly. 'Toad in the Hole! I'll give you Toad in the Hole!'

'Thank you,' said Olga primly, 'but I happen to be a strict vegetarian.'

'"Toad in the Hole,"' spluttered Noel, 'is what human beings call *sausage in batter*.'

Olga looked from one to the other of her friends.

'Well,' she said at last, 'if the Sawdust people will give things silly names like that they must expect misunderstandings. Why, they might just as well call a dish "Guinea-pig in the Hole" . . .'

'That,' said Noel, as he turned away in disgust, 'is something that can always be arranged, and one of these days most likely will. Goodnight!'

CHAPTER TEN

Olga and the Chinese Dragon

Although Olga had lived with the Sawdust family for quite a long time – almost a year in fact, and although there was much that she'd come to take for granted, there was one thing she never grew tired of – and that was the view from her hutch.

The memory of her early days in the pet shop had grown hazy, but if she tried hard she could still picture what it had been like cooped up with all the other animals, and often when she looked out of her bedroom window she felt very lucky, for there was always something interesting going on.

The Sawdust family's house was perched on the side of a hill and from her own house she could see right across the valley. There were houses dotting the hill on the far side too, and in the evening, when the lights were on, they looked like fireflies twinkling amongst the trees. On really dark nights there were so many lights it was impossible to count them all. Olga had once got up to five, but then she became confused, and by the time she'd gone back over them again it was late and some were already being turned off.

The view was equally pretty in the daytime, and from her window she was able to watch in comfort the gradual coming and going of the seasons; the long winter months when the ground was covered with snow and people slid down the hillside on sleighs and toboggans, their whoops of joy echoing across the valley; and the coming of spring, when the whole countryside changed from brown to green.

In many ways Olga liked the spring, for it meant fresh grass and other delicacies; but the most beautiful mornings of all were undoubtedly those when the whole valley was filled with mist, and it felt as if she was looking down on some vast and mysterious sea of cotton wool. This took place mostly in autumn and early spring, but sometimes, when the weather was in a particular mood, it happened in summer too.

It was on just such a day that she chanced to overhear a remark passed by one of the neighbours as Karen Sawdust went in search of some early-morning dandelions.

'It's real dragon weather this morning,' she called over the fence.

'Dragon weather?' Karen Sawdust's voice floated back.

'In China,' explained the lady, 'they say dragons come out of the mist on mornings like this.'

The voices faded away leaving Olga busy with her thoughts. She peered out through her door in the hope of seeing something unusual. But not a ripple disturbed the scene below, and the only sound came from a building site down in the valley as the men started work for the day.

The building site, from all Olga could gather, was a bit of a thorn in the flesh of the Sawdust family. It seemed that some land had recently been sold and some new houses were being built. They were unlikely to spoil the view, for they were below the skyline, but it did mean a shattering of the normal peace and quiet for the time being as trees and hedges were uprooted, and strange things called concrete mixers and bulldozers began to arrive.

'Perhaps,' said Olga to herself, 'a dragon will come

and gobble them all up before they've finished.'

She made the remark almost without thinking, and it had hardly left her lips when her eyes grew wide with astonishment. For a second or two she sat transfixed, unable to move let alone utter a squeak. For there, rising out of the mist, was an enormous giraffe-necked creature the like of which she'd never seen before. A long thin tongue emerged from its tiny head and swung gently to and fro as if in search of something, and then, ever so slowly, it disappeared from view again.

'I see they have a crane on the building site now.' Karen Sawdust's voice brought Olga back to earth with a jolt.

'Let's hope it gets the job finished twice as quickly,' said her mother. 'It's been going on long enough.'

'A crane!' Olga sank back into her hay. For a moment, for one dreadful moment, she'd thought it was a dragon. She felt very pleased she'd found out the truth of the matter, and she felt doubly thankful some while later when she was put out in her run on the lawn. Goodness knows how she would have felt if she hadn't known what it was. She looked around to see who else was about, but the only sign of life came from the direction of the rockery, where Graham was basking in the early morning sunshine, and *he* wouldn't have been much good in an emergency – especially when it came to fighting dragons.

The top of the crane came and went several times and Olga began playing a game with herself as she set about clearing the patch of grass. She made up a spell which she timed to say just before the crane rose into view. Then she made up another one to send it away again.

She was so busy doing this she didn't notice Fangio creeping up on her and she had quite a turn when he spoke.

'Are you all right?' he asked.

'Of course I'm all right,' replied Olga crossly.

'I thought I heard you talking to someone,' said Fangio.

'Where are you going?' asked Olga, quickly changing the subject.

'Oh, into the bushes,' said Fangio vaguely. 'I might go up the hill. On the other hand, I might go down it. I shall have to see how the fancy takes me.'

Olga looked at him thoughtfully as he turned to go. 'I wouldn't go down into the valley if I were you,' she called. 'Not while the dragon is about.'

Fangio stopped in his tracks. 'Dragon?' he repeated. 'What dragon?'

'Haven't you heard?' asked Olga carelessly. 'Everyone's out looking for it. It's been loose in the valley all the morning, and it's *very* hungry.

'It's a Chinese dragon,' she added in a louder voice for Graham's benefit. 'As tall as a house and with a roar that shakes the ground. It lives on a diet of hedgehogs and tortoises, with,' she added as she spotted Noel coming across the lawn, 'an occasional mog thrown in when it feels like a treat.'

'What's this? What's this?' Noel broke off his wanderings to join them.

Graham stuck his head out of his shell. 'There's a dragon loose in the valley,' he called. 'It's eating all before it. Better pass the word around quickly.'

Noel stared at Olga. 'It sounds to me like another of your tales,' he said suspiciously. 'If there really was a dragon, I can't picture you sitting there as calm as a cucumber for a start.'

Olga drew herself up. 'It just so happens,' she said haughtily, 'that the one thing all dragons are frightened of is guinea-pigs.

'We guinea-pigs,' she continued, lowering her voice, 'have magic powers over dragons. We can make them come and go as we please.'

'I shall believe that,' said Noel, 'when I see it.'

'All right!' Olga put on one of her expressions. 'I take a nibble of clover, and a morsel or two of grass, and I add a pinch of dandelion, then I say a few things that have been handed down . . .' she waited for the rattle of the crane and then, as it started to rise, she made a series of strange grunting noises, running round and round in circles as she did so.

The others sat petrified as the top of the crane rose into view. This time it had a big platform laden with bricks hanging from its 'tongue'.

'It *must* be hungry,' said Olga carelessly. 'Would you like me to make it go away again – just in case?'

'Yes, please!' called Graham, from somewhere inside his shell. 'I don't like it.'

Olga took a deep breath, 'Go away, dragon!' she cried. 'We do not like you. Go away before it is too late. Wheeeee!'

Olga timed it exactly right, for just as she gave her 'wheeeee' the crane lowered the platform into a

new position and disappeared from view again.

The others stared at her in amazement, and for once even Noel could hardly find the right words.

'You never told us you could do that before!' he gasped.

'You didn't ask me,' said Olga. She turned her back on the others and carried on with her eating. 'There are so many things I can do I daresay there are quite a few I've forgotten to mention. If you like I'll do it for you again.' And closing her eyes she went through her grunting noises once more.

A movement somewhere behind him caused Noel to look round. Almost immediately he arched his back. 'That was quick,' he said.

Olga had a momentary feeling of surprise, for she'd missed the usual rattle that meant the crane was going up. 'My dragon spells,' she said, 'are very powerful. It'll probably keep coming back for quite a while. But don't worry, I can always make it go away again.'

'I wish you'd make it go away now then,' cried Fangio, his beady eyes agog. 'I don't like the look of it close to. It's bigger . . . and more fierce . . . and . . .'

Something in the tone of Fangio's voice made Olga look round too. As she did so she nearly jumped out of her skin with fright, for she suddenly caught sight of an enormous green head with a yellow mouth and

large staring eyes heading towards them across the lawn.

'Quick. Do one of your spells,' hissed Noel, as the head rose into the air and bore down on them. 'Do something!'

'Wheeeeeeeeeee!' shrieked Olga. 'Wheeeeeeeee! Wheeeeeeeeeeeee! Wheeeeeeeeeeeeeeeee! Help! Help! Wheeeeeeeeeeeeeeeeeeeeeeeeeeeeeee!'

Olga knew exactly what she was going to do and she did it with all possible speed. Regardless of the terrified cries from the others, she made a dive for the back of her run and buried her face in the corner as far as it could possibly go. She was conscious of the fact that she could hear a voice calling her name and that it was getting nearer and nearer, but she was much too scared to see who it was. There were times when closing your eyes and burying your head was the only possible thing to do and this was definitely one of them.

Karen Sawdust looked down at Olga's run. Really, animals were the strangest creatures. There was no telling how they were going to behave. Noel had scudded past her like a streak of greased lightning. Fangio hadn't been far behind. Even Graham had shown a surprising turn of speed as he'd disappeared into the shrubbery. And now Olga was acting in an equally odd manner. Anyone would think they'd come face to face with a real dragon.

'It's all right,' she said, holding up a large object on the end of a string. 'It won't do you any harm. It's only made of wood and paper. It's a Chinese kite. The lady next door lent it to me. Anyway, there isn't enough wind to fly it . . .'

But she might just as well have saved her breath, for if Olga did hear what she was saying it had no effect. She was past caring what the object was made of. Wood, paper, string . . . it was all the same to her. She would never, ever, say her dragon spell again.

CHAPTER ELEVEN

A Day to Remember

The meeting with the dragon left Olga feeling decidedly queasy for several days afterwards. At first it didn't bother her a great deal. After all, it wasn't every day one met a dragon, and it would probably never happen again. But as the days multiplied and she still didn't feel any better she began to wonder if it really was that. The early mornings were the worst. She didn't actually feel bad, just off-colour, and somehow slightly 'different'. Then there was the matter of food. It wasn't that she was off food, it was simply that she was forever wanting things that weren't there. If her run was put on a patch where there were plenty of dandelions she had a craving for clover. If it was put on top of of the clover she suddenly had a great desire for dandelions.

And there was the strange affair of THE NOTICE. It appeared one day on the front of her house; a piece of cardboard tied on with string across the front door. In some ways Olga rather liked it, for it made her more private and she suddenly felt the need to be by herself. But she was dying to know what it said, and she knew that it said *something*, for she caught sight of some words later that morning on her way back from the lawn.

But even her visits to the outside run suddenly stopped for some reason or other, so she had to rely on her friends – and they weren't much help.

With Fangio inclined to be short-sighted, and Graham having no idea how to read, it was left to Noel, and that evening he climbed up onto her roof in order to take a closer look.

Peering over the edge, he announced that the piece of cardboard said 'BRUTSID TON OD'.

It took him some while to work even that much out, for he was seeing the letters upside down and had to read them out one by one.

Olga played around with them for ages afterwards,

but she couldn't make any sense out of it at all, so in the end she gave it up as a bad job and contented herself with the thought that if you wait long enough most things have a habit of becoming clear in the end.

Then, a few days later, several things happened one after another. Things that were to make it a day to remember.

It all began when the postman arrived. Olga had often seen him before, but only in the distance, for he usually went to the Sawdust family's front door. The moment he arrived he was grabbed by Karen Sawdust and ushered round to the back of the house where he dipped into his bag and brought out six large envelopes for Olga to see.

'Morning,' he said gruffly. 'Happy birthday!'

'Happy birthday?' Olga stopped munching and gazed out of her front door in amazement. Fancy it being her *birthday* and she hadn't even realized.

'There's a card from Mummy and Daddy,' said Karen Sawdust, as Mr and Mrs Sawdust came out to join in the fun. She tore open the envelope and withdrew a piece of folded cardboard with a picture on the front.

'There's one from me,' she continued, tearing open the next envelope.

'One from Noel . . .

'One from Fangio . . .

'One from Graham . . .

'And one from Boris. I don't suppose you remember *him*. He was the guinea-pig you stayed with earlier in the year.' She cast a meaning glance at the others. 'And in the circumstances I think sending you a card is the least he can do!'

'Boris!' Olga could hardly believe her ears. Fancy asking if she remembered him! To start with he was the only other guinea-pig she'd seen in months, so she could hardly *forget* him. But it wasn't *just* that. There'd been something special about her week-end with Boris that would have made him stay in her mind if she'd met a thousand others.

And then she pricked up her ears at something else Karen Sawdust was saying.

'He'll be here soon,' she said. 'They told us they would leave early. They're coming to stay for a whole week! Gosh. Wouldn't it be super if it all happened together!'

Boris! Coming to stay! With her! For a whole week! Sometime that very morning! Soon! Any moment now!

'Wheeeeeeeeee!' Olga ran round and round her house squeaking with excitement at the thought, until she suddenly had one of her dizzy spells.

'Oh dear,' she thought, 'I do hope I'm well enough to receive him.'

Olga's dizzy spell lasted longer than usual, but she roused herself quickly enough when the sound of a car engine heralded the moment she'd been waiting for.

Even then there were endless moments of chattering to be endured, but at long last the voices drew nearer and a familiar set of whiskers came into view.

'Hullo,' said Boris, as the door closed behind him. 'How are you? I see you've got your DO NOT DISTURB notice. What a thing to have hanging up on your birthday. Still, it can't be helped.' He looked at her critically. 'I hope you've got plenty of oats. It won't be long now before you've a few more mouths to feed.'

'A few more mouths to feed?' Olga looked at him incredulously as she suddenly realized the truth of the matter; the reason why she'd been feeling so strange for the past few days. What a ridiculous thing! And fancy not being able to work out that 'BRUTSID TON OD' was 'DO NOT DISTURB' backwards. Obviously the Sawdust family suspected something, otherwise they wouldn't have put the notice up in the first place. That was why they'd been fussing over her more than usual – not letting her go in her outside run. And all the time she'd hadn't suspected a thing! Really, she began to feel quite flustered.

Of course, the trouble was that what with one thing and another – going to the sea-side, detecting, thinking up new stories, rescuing Venables, swimming, not to mention making dragon spells, she'd been so busy she hadn't had time to think about anything.

'I really must pay more attention to myself in future,' she decided. 'I'm always doing things for others.'

'It's a good job I got here in time!' Boris broke into her thoughts. He looked round carefully and then moved a little closer. 'You might not think it to look at me,' he murmured, 'but I was once a very famous surgeon. If you like, I'll tell you a story about one of my operations.'

Olga gazed at him happily. As far as she was concerned Boris could go on telling stories for the rest of her life. She wouldn't believe a word, but she would never grow tired of hearing them.

It was a little later that same morning that she suddenly noticed a tiny movement inside her.

'I think you'd better finish your story later,' she said hastily. 'I may be busy for a while.'

Olga was true to her word. For the rest of that morning she was very busy indeed, and as she lay back at long last and looked down happily at the three small figures poking out from under the straw and felt them nuzzle up to her, she decided she was likely to remain busy for some time to come.

There was great excitement in the Sawdust family household when they heard the news. First Karen Sawdust, then Mr and Mrs Sawdust came to see her. There then followed a long procession of friends and neighbours. It went on for most of the day.

And to cap it all, there was still one more surprise in store for her.

Later that same evening Karen Sawdust headed yet another procession from the house. This time she was carrying a small, white object on a plate, and on top of it there was a lighted candle.

Olga gave a squeak of surprise. Whatever was going to happen to her now?

'It's to celebrate your birthday,' explained Karen Sawdust, as she drew near. 'You're one year old today. The cake's only made out of cardboard, I'm afraid; but if you nibble a hole in the side you'll find it's full of oats. And if you blow the candle out in one blow you can make a wish – which *may* come true.'

Olga had no idea how to blow, but she gave a loud 'wheeeeeee' instead, and with some help from the others the flame went out.

There was a round of applause and some cheering, and then all the Sawdust people sang 'Happy birthday, dear Olga, happy birthday to you.'

Olga didn't want to seem ungrateful, but by then she was feeling so tired she decided to wish that they would all go away, and lo and behold shortly afterwards they did. Only Noel, Fangio and Graham, drawn by all the noise, remained to say goodnight.

Olga snuggled up to Boris. One way and another it

had been quite a day – a day to remember. 'How nice to have furs and descendants,' she sighed, gazing proudly at her three offspring.

'Don't you mean *heirs* and descendants?' called Noel, who liked to get these things right.

Olga roused herself. 'No, I do not,' she said firmly, '*You've* never seen a guinea-pig with hair. They *always* have fur. Beautiful soft, silky, lovely fur . . .'

'Goodnight!' said Noel hastily.

'Goodnight!' echoed Fangio and Graham.

And from somewhere near the kitchen door there came a loud croak.

'Goodnight, Venables,' said Olga.

She settled down again next to Boris and closed her eyes. 'If you like,' she said graciously, 'you may tell us a story now. I've had such a busy day I don't think I could possibly manage one myself. Besides, it's a father's privilege!'

DO NOT DISTURB